THE WAVERING WEREWOLF

Look for the other exciting titles in

THE ACCIDENTAL MONSTERS series:

THE VANISHING VAMPIRE

THE UNWILLING WITCH

David Lubar

AN
APPLE
PAPERBACK

SCHOLASTIC INC.
New York Toronto London Auckland Sydney

ISBN 0-590-90720-4

12 11 10 9 8 7 6 5 4 3 2 1   7 8 9/9 0 1 2/0

Printed in the U.S.A.   40
First Scholastic printing, December 1997

For Jack and Yvonne, who always believed in me

CONTENTS

THE WAVERING WEREWOLF

CHAPTER
1
ON THE NOSE

I belong in the woods about as much as a tennis ball belongs in a frying pan. It was absolutely ridiculous for me to be walking along a nature trail, looking at all the marvels that are to be found in the great outdoors. If I want to see a spotted tiger moth, I'll examine it under a microscope, thank you. But our class was on a field trip, and there was no reasonable way I could get out of going. The trip counted toward our grade. If there's one thing I treasure, it's my grades. How else can I keep score?

So, there I was, lagging at the back of the group following Mr. Rubinitsky along the high trail through Miller Forest, soaking up all the beauty and glory of several thousand plants, half of which were capable of making me sneeze, the other half of which were capable of giving me a skin rash. Ah, nature! And lag I did, falling farther and farther behind as I stopped to examine potential specimens. Despite my extreme dislike of the outdoors, I figured there was no reason to waste an observation opportunity. And there were several species of fungi that were extremely interesting. It's funny how most people don't even realize what a fascinating life-form fungi are.

So that is how, despite being on a clearly marked trail under the supervision of a professional teacher, I managed to get lost in the woods. I had stopped to examine a particularly alluring variety of fungus and was wondering whether to take a spore sample for later study when I looked up and noticed that I was the only large mammal in sight. One moment, I'm a student, the next, I'm Hansel. I got up and dashed ahead, but the path forked.

"Hey!" I shouted. I listened for a reply. There was none. Now, I was faced with three choices.

One: I could stay right where I was and hope they noticed I was missing. That didn't seem like a practical solution. I'd never been missed in my life. If I had been Adam, I could have left the garden for weeks and weeks without Eve realizing something was different.

Two: I could choose a path and follow it. Since one path was right and one was wrong, that approach had a fifty-percent chance of returning me to my classmates. Not the best odds, but at least I could put a number on it. Of course, if the path forked again, the odds would get worse.

Three: I could head back the way we'd come and meet the others by the bus. That was assuming I could find my way back. An amusing assumption — I've been known to get lost walking home from school.

I was sure there were other possibilities, but I also knew that the longer I waited before making a choice, the more unknown factors would intrude. Before I could make my decision, I was distracted by a frantic rustling. A small creature dashed across the path, skittering out of the woods on one side of the trail, then back in on the other side. I caught just enough of a glimpse to know it was a rabbit. I stepped to the edge of the path and stared at the spot where the animal had run.

That's when I heard the growl.

Actually, it was more of a snarl. Well, it was sort of a half-snarl half-growl sound. The differences probably weren't important at the moment. The key feature here was the threatening nature of the sound. This was not some form of animal greeting or mating call. This sounded more like "Hello, lunch."

I took off, picking the more active half of the fight-or-flight reaction, and started stumbling from the path and through the woods. Some small part of my mind was amused that I seemed to be choosing the same route as the rabbit. The rest of my mind was busy urging my body to move faster. Running is not my best activity, but I must say I achieved a new personal record as I tore through the underbrush.

Unfortunately, whatever was chasing me had a lot more experience in this version of tag. The growling sounds got closer. They were right behind me. Then they were right on me. Something slammed into my back.

I went earthward face forward. The force made me roll right over. It was the first time in my life I had ever done a somersault. I didn't like it. As I slammed to a stop, my glasses bounced from my head. I panicked at the thought of losing them, but I got lucky. When I groped through the leaves that surrounded me, I felt the frames right away.

Before I could put on my glasses or stand up, something gray and sleek and fast landed on my chest. It was so close to me that it was mostly a blur, but it was a blur with a mouth and a tongue and teeth — especially teeth. Even without my glasses, I could tell that the blurry teeth ended in blurry points of the kind designed to make holes in just about anything. The teeth appeared about ready to bite my face. This wasn't a good thing.

I raised my hand as the animal lunged closer, the mouth so wide it looked like my whole head would disappear inside. A wave of hot, raw animal breath washed over me.

"Norman!"

The shouts from the path must have startled it. The head jerked back as the jaws snapped shut.

"Yeeyouch!" It nipped my nose. Then it leaped away from me. With one powerful spring, it hurtled far off through the underbrush. I put on my glasses and looked toward the side in time to catch the quickest glimpse of something gray and fast. It was gone before I could determine what it was. It seemed to move through the woods with barely a sound.

"Norman!" More voices joined the search. The footsteps came closer.

"Here!" I shouted, carefully feeling my face to see if my glasses still had a nose to lean on. Ick. My head was pretty well slobbered up, but my nose seemed okay, though it was a bit sore at the tip.

With all this going on, the oddest thing is how only one aspect remained clear in my mind from that moment. Despite all that had just happened, I mostly could recall a tiny sensation that, at the time, seemed unimportant. My palms itched. They itched fiercely.

CHAPTER
2

LYING IN THE WOODS

Sebastian was the first one to reach me. Everyone calls him Splat for a rather silly reason. It's a tale best saved for another time. The rest of the class wasn't far behind. They all managed to crowd around and stare at me like I was some sort of traffic accident that had suddenly appeared in the middle of the woods, and not just a kid who was lying on his back amid the greenery. People's faces look really odd when you're lying on the ground looking up. Everyone becomes mostly nostrils and lips.

"Norman, where'd you go?" Splat asked.

I looked around. Why do people ask such silly questions? It was obvious where I went. I went right to the spot where I was. But I didn't answer him. Part of me still wasn't thinking clearly. There's something about being chased like a bunny through the woods that gets in the way of calm thought.

"Are you okay?" Dawn asked, stepping forward from the mob. Despite carrying the burdens of being both extremely pretty and extremely popular, she somehow managed to also be extremely nice.

"Yeah, thanks. I'm fine." I sat up and, realizing that I needed some excuse for being flat out on the ground, pointed over my head toward the branches. "Fractal designs," I said.

Mr. Rubinitsky had joined us. "What's that, Norman?"

"Fractals," I said again. "Look at the branching patterns of the trees. It's a classic example of fractals. You know, repeated patterns that get smaller and smaller. Branches, crystals, shorelines, that sort of thing." Kids started to drift away. Mr. Rubinitsky hung in, but I knew that he'd only last for a few more sentences. "I was trying to observe the exact structure of the branches, and the best position seemed to be the one in which you found me. It's quite fascinating, really, the way that —"

"Okay, okay, just don't wander off again," Mr. Rubinitsky said as he gathered the class and headed back toward the trail.

I couldn't help letting a small smile slip onto my lips. The best way to avoid attention was to talk about what interested me. It worked like magic.

"Fractals?" Splat whispered as we left the woods. He gave me a grin that showed he knew my trick. "What were you really doing?"

I wouldn't have told anyone else, but Splat and I had been through a lot together. I thought back to the sleek gray shape. It could only have been one thing. "A wolf was chasing me," I said. "It knocked me down, and I'm fairly positive it was about to dine on various portions of my body."

"Or maybe it just wanted the basket of goodies you were taking to Grandma," Splat said.

"Very funny. I'm serious. It was definitely a wolf."

Splat shrugged. "Whatever you say." Then he stared at my face. "Oh, gross. Did you know you're bleeding?"

I touched the tip of my nose. All I felt was a small scratch. "That's where the wolf bit me."

"Yeah." Sebastian nodded. "I saw that on television. Wolves always bring down their prey by the nose. It's a standard hunting technique. Once you've got control of the nose, the body has to follow. That's why wolves are so good at hunting elephants." He laughed.

I sighed. Splat was my friend, but he didn't take me very seriously. "Hey, I think Dawn was smiling at you," I told him.

"Really?" Ever since she'd stopped trying to get his attention last year, he'd started noticing her. But she pretty much acted like he didn't exist.

I nodded. Splat looked up toward the front of the line where Dawn was, then asked, "You mind?"

"Nope. Go right ahead."

He ran to catch up with her. I felt a little guilty about telling him something that wasn't true, but I wanted to walk by myself for a while. I wasn't in the mood for his jokes. It was bad enough to have the whole class find me lying in the middle of the woods. Of course, this one small incident wouldn't make much of a difference in the way I was treated by my fellow students. Most of the kids already thought I was a bit on the strange side.

They didn't understand me. They didn't understand that I was interested in *everything*. I just loved learning new facts and knowing about all kinds of things. For some reason, they thought this was peculiar. As a result, nothing I could do would surprise them. I guess nothing I did would surprise me, either. At least, that's what I thought. It's funny how quickly things can change.

CHAPTER

3

JUMPING TO CONCLUSIONS

*T*he bus ride back to school went fairly smoothly. One or two kids made jokes about me. Then someone asked if I was taking up cloud watching. Someone else said I'd finally found the perfect spot to hang out. There were a few other comments, all equally lacking in humor. Well, to me they were lacking in humor. To everyone else on the bus, they must have seemed funny since there was a lot of laughter. Had it happened to someone else, I would have made a comment like "Hey, congratulations on your new position." But nobody would have gotten the joke, even though it's pretty obvious that when you lie down, you end up in a different position than when you're standing. As it was, I just ignored them and looked out the window. Slowly, the woods gave way to shops and houses and other signs of civilization.

After a while, Splat plunked down in the seat

next to me. He'd been at the back of the bus with the cool kids, trying to get Dawn's attention. Apparently, he'd failed again. We weren't supposed to walk around when the bus is moving, but that doesn't stop Splat.

"Hey, Wolfgang," he said, grinning.

"Want to do something after school?" I asked him, ignoring the feeble joke.

"Sure. How about a movie?"

"Sounds good. I don't have too much homework, so we can make the early show." There was a new picture playing in town — *Return of the Brain-Sucking Leech People*. I'd never seen the first *Leech People* film, but that didn't matter. It was just something to help pass the afternoon. Splat and I both preferred the older movies, the classics like the original versions of *Frankenstein* and *Dracula*. Some of the best and scariest movies I had ever seen were the old black-and-white ones. But the new stuff was okay to help kill an afternoon.

The bus rolled into the lot at the side of the school and we got off. We went inside to be dismissed, then left the building. I walked with Splat toward our part of town until we reached the corner of Maple and Spruce where I had to turn off for my house. "See ya," I said as we split.

"Bye." Then he howled like a wolf and laughed.

I swear, despite the fact that he's my friend, he can be a real pain sometimes. He probably doesn't even know how his comments make me feel. I went the final two blocks toward home. On the way, I felt my nose again. There was a scratch, but it didn't seem bad. As I went up the front steps, I could smell something wonderful coming from inside. I realized Mom must have gotten an order. She works as a caterer, making food for parties and weddings and other occasions. She's such a good cook that I sometimes wonder why I don't weigh three hundred pounds. Now there's a frightening thought. That would really kill what little social life I have. I guess I'm just lucky.

"Is that you, Norman?" she asked when I came in.

"Nope," I said, strolling into the kitchen. "It must be someone else who just happened to walk in at the very same time your dear son usually comes home from a hard day of school. I'm a professional Norman impersonator. This is how I make my living." Sometimes my mouth gets ahead of my brain. Or maybe my mouth and brain just get ahead of my judgment. Either way, I end up sounding like a wise guy far more often than would be wise.

Mom barely looked up from the pot she was stirring. "Well, whoever you are, would you like a taste?" She understands me — or she's just used to me.

"Sure." I took a taste.

It was good. It was always good. Mom could close her eyes, grab two or three things from the fridge, and make an incredible meal. She just had that gift. As for me, I'm not allowed to use the oven anymore after that time I tried to create a new type of plastic. It didn't work out quite the way I expected. But that's another long story that's too painful to remember.

"Beef?" I asked.

Mom shook her head. "Nope. It's lamb with curry. Very Indian."

"Very delicious, too." I took another taste, then went up to my room. There was something I had to check out. I pulled down my book on North American mammals. Yup, just as I'd thought, there were no wolves in this area. Their range didn't come within five hundred miles of here. That left several explanations. Most likely, the creature was an escaped pet, or an abandoned animal. That would explain why it hadn't gone completely wild when it attacked me. Perhaps it had escaped from a zoo. But then there'd be something on the news. That would be easy enough to find out. I powered up my computer and logged into our account. Dad gets free Net access through the college where he teaches. I went to several news sites and searched the headlines for the keyword *wolf*. I found nothing.

I stopped surfing and turned my attention to scratching. My neck itched. It felt almost like I had just gotten a haircut. I flipped off the computer and dragged my books out of my backpack so I could do my homework.

"Just a pet, not a wild wolf," I said as I started to work. My stomach growled in agreement.

I opened my math book to the page with the homework problems. Even though it was nothing difficult, I enjoyed it. I've always liked numbers. They're almost as much fun as toys, in their own way. Take my phone number for example. The last four digits are 2816. Now, at a glance, there's nothing special. But two times eight is sixteen. Two, eight, sixteen. I think that's interesting. Splat's number is 3924. Three times three is nine, and two times two is four, so each number is followed by its square. I think that's extremely cool. I'd love to trade phone numbers with him.

Outside my window, I could see a squirrel running down the tree by the side of the driveway.

I started doing the homework problems. The first question involved two planes moving at different speeds.

The squirrel left the trunk and crawled onto a large branch. It looked around, then moved carefully toward the middle of the branch.

I calculated the distance covered by the first plane. It was simple: Distance equals speed multiplied by time. There was a rattling wooden clack as the pencil slipped from my fingers and hit the desk. I stood and walked, slowly, silently, toward the window. My feet met the floor with less than a whisper.

The squirrel, ten feet away from the house, swished its tail and took another step.

Carefully, I slid the window open and removed the

screen. I had not yet made the slightest sound other than a faint scraping as the screen slid free. My mind flicked to the next part of the problem. The second plane had gone half the distance of the first, so the answer was obvious.

The squirrel sensed something. It looked toward me. Its body tensed, preparing for a dash to safety. The tail lifted and twitched.

Where was my pencil? I should write down the answer.

The squirrel turned its head. Our eyes met. I held the creature as our gazes locked. For a moment, it froze. But its need to survive was strong. The squirrel broke from the grip of my stare. I knew it would run back toward the trunk in an instant. I had to make my move now, or I would lose the chance.

I leaped.

4

HANGING OUT

I suspect my lack of athletic ability saved my neck. If I'd had any coordination at all, the leap would have carried me right out the window. There's no way I could have reached the tree. Even the greatest athlete in the world couldn't have made that jump. Luckily, I'm a bit of a klutz. Actually, I'm a lot of a klutz. My leap, to use a term far grander than the motion deserved, carried me up a foot or so and partway out of the window. Unfortunately, it carried me far enough out that I fell through the opening.

Some instinct made me spread my legs. I spread them wide enough to hook my feet around the corners of the window. That brought my fall to a jolting stop, but there was no way I could get back in. There was no way I wanted to drop to the ground, either.

Quite simply, I was stuck.

It was not a comfortable position. The blood was starting to rush to my head. My legs were beginning to get cramps and my glasses had swung past my forehead. Several coins bounced off my ear as they slipped from my pocket. They struck with tiny clinks against the small stones in the flower bed below me. I thought about spending the next few months with both arms in plaster casts. It didn't seem very promising.

"Hey, you in that much of a hurry for a movie?"

I looked down at the top of Splat's head. Without my glasses in front of my eyes, everything was mostly a fuzzy blur, but I recognized his voice. This seemed to be my day for seeing heads from different angles. "I slipped," I said.

"Need some help?"

"That would be nice. Do you think you could avoid mentioning my current predicament to my mom?" I knew that parents tended to worry about safety. If Mom saw me dangling like this, she'd probably have all the windows in the house removed.

"No problem. I'll be right up."

I watched the top of his blurry head move toward the door. I knew he'd have no trouble. Mom would let him right in. She liked Splat. Just about everybody liked him. He was fun to have around. When he grows up, it wouldn't surprise me if he became a senator or an actor or something like that.

There was a brief delay, during which I worked very hard on not slipping farther out the window. Finally, a pair of hands gripped my ankles.

"Hang on," he said. "I've got you."

A moment later, I was back in my room. It felt good to be right-side up. I replaced the screen and flexed my leg muscles to get rid of the cramps.

"Care to explain?" Splat asked.

"Nope," I said, shrugging.

"Come on, what were you doing?"

I walked over to the shelf that ran along the wall opposite my bed and took down one of my specimen jars — the one with the bees. "Have I shown you these? I just collected them last month. All the stingers are intact." That was pretty mean of me. I knew Splat hated bugs, and I usually didn't do this sort of thing, but I wasn't sure what had happened and I didn't want to talk about it.

"Well, let's get going," he said, backing away from me and the bees. "The movie starts in half an hour."

"I can't wait to see it," I said, putting the jar back on the shelf.

As we headed toward town, I tried to understand what I'd done. I knew I'd sat down to start my homework. And I knew I'd ended up hanging out the window. It was the part in between that was unclear. I'd seen a squirrel. And I'd risen to get a better look at it. Then I'd gone to the window. Had I jumped at the squirrel? No, that's not right. I would never have attempted a stunt like that. I must have tripped or something.

By the time we reached the corner, I'd given up trying to figure out what had happened. As long as it didn't happen again, it really didn't matter. Right now, I had a date with some brain-sucking leech people.

On the way into town, we saw something else that got us talking. Stapled to a phone pole — stapled to *many* phone poles, we soon discovered — was a poster announcing the arrival of THE HULL BROTHERS' CIRCUS: THREE RINGS OF THRILLS, CHILLS, AND YET EVEN MORE THRILLS.

"Sounds great," Splat said, pausing in front of the pole. "I really like the circus."

"I hope their performers are better than their posters." I looked more closely at the advertisement. Actually, except for the rather weak headline, it wasn't all that bad. There were colorful pictures of trapeze artists and high-wire walkers, along with an elephant, some horses, and lots of clowns. At the bottom of the poster, it said: SEE THE ELEPHANTS, SEE THE HORSES, SEE THE MONKEY BOY.

"Come on," Splat said, "we'll miss the beginning of the movie." He started jogging down the street.

I followed, dropping a bit behind. If I run too much, my glasses start slipping down my nose. I hate that. But I wasn't sure whether Splat would wait for me at the ticket booth or go inside without me. If he went inside, I'd have a hard time finding him in the dark.

Sure enough, by the time I reached the ticket window, Splat was nowhere in sight. I bought my ticket and went in, hoping I could spot him before he sat down.

But it wasn't as dark in the theater as usual. I found him right away — halfway down the theater on the left. The movie hadn't begun yet, so I went to the snack counter and got some popcorn, a box of gummy eyes, and a root beer.

I reached my seat just as the film started. "Aren't they going to shut off the lights?" I asked as I sat down.

Splat turned toward me, a puzzled expression on his face. "What do you mean?"

I rubbed my eyes. It was dark, I guess, but it didn't seem as dark as normal. "Nothing," I said. Then I dug into my snacks and settled down to watch the leech people suck the brains out of almost everyone in an unsuspecting town. All in all, it promised to be a satisfying afternoon. It would have been perfect if it hadn't been for a little problem with the idiot behind me.

CHAPTER 5

HUSH

I hate it when people talk during a movie. It was just my luck that I had ended up one row in front of someone who must have been trying to become the King of the Movie Talkers. He jabbered and chattered and babbled without any sign of ever stopping. If a leech person appeared, he'd say, "Look, a leech person." If someone was about to walk into a room where a leech person was hiding, he'd say, "Don't go in, there's a leech person."

The talking by itself would have been enough to annoy me. What made it even worse was that the comments were so stupid they were driving me out of my mind.

About halfway through the movie, I snapped. It wasn't like me. Usually, I take whatever the world dumps on me in relative silence. I've had a lot of practice.

This time, I really lost it.

I turned around and shouted, "SHUT UP! JUST SHUT UP! PLEASE, PLEASE, PLEASE SHUT UP, YOU IDIOT!" My eyes scrunch up when I shout. If they'd been open, I would have been the one who'd kept his mouth shut. When I finally got a good look, I suddenly understood how a turkey feels on Thanksgiving morning. The kid sitting behind me was huge. He looked like a rock with arms.

He didn't say a word. For one long moment he just stared at me with a confused expression. I could almost hear his brain clicking as the various facts of the situation forced their attention on him. As painful as thinking must have been for him, I could see he had figured out the correct response to my shouts. All at once, he looked like he had made a decision. He pulled his foot back, then shot it forward and kicked my seat.

I felt like a bowling pin. It's amazing my bones didn't go flying right out of my body. After the kick, he said, "I'm gonna get you."

I looked over at Splat. "Maybe we should move," I said.

"Good idea."

We slipped from our seats. As I hurried away, I kept waiting for a huge hand to grab me by the shoulder and fling me through the air. Or maybe he would squeeze me like an accordion, playing music while he crushed various parts of my body.

But we made it out of the aisle and across the theater to the other side.

"That was not a healthy thing to do," Splat whispered after we took our new seats.

"Who was that?" I didn't recognize my new enemy.

"Got to be a Mellon," Splat said.

"Yeah." I nodded. The Mellons were born big. Lud and Bud Mellon went to our school. They had a lot of relatives. They used to be pretty mean, but had calmed down a bit recently.

"Speak of the devils," Splat said, looking toward the entrance.

I watched as Lud and Bud came into the theater and walked up to the talker. "Sorry we're late, Cousin Spud," Lud said.

I turned to Splat and said, "Spud Mellon?"

"What?" Splat asked.

"They called him 'Cousin Spud.' "

Behind us, someone said, "Hey, quit talking. We're trying to watch a movie. What's wrong with you? Ain't you got no manners? Stupid kids . . ."

I slunk down in my seat and tried to enjoy the rest of the movie. I hoped that Cousin Spud would forget about me — a likely action for a Mellon — or not recognize me the next time we met. If it was dark, I'd have a chance, but the theater was so much lighter than usual that I had little hope of being saved by the dimness of the room. I'd just have to depend instead on the dimness of the Mellons.

Still, I had yelled at someone much bigger and sur-vived. That should have made me feel wonderful, given how few victories I've experienced in the phys-ical world. But all I could think about was what would happen if he decided to carry out his threat. On top of that, my neck started itching. I scratched, enjoying how fabulous my nails felt against my skin. They seemed longer and sharper than usual. I guess I'd neglected to cut them recently. That was odd. I usually paid great attention to personal grooming.

My back itched, too.

HERE'S LOOKING AT YOU

"Well, I think I'll go home and tell Rory about the movie," Splat said as the film ended. "Want to come?"

I knew he liked to share the stories with his little brother. Rory wasn't allowed to see horror movies, but Splat always gave him a mild version of the story so the kid would feel he'd been there with us. I liked Rory — he was a lot of fun for a miniature person — but I felt a need to be by myself. "I think I'll head home," I said.

"Okay, see you tomorrow." Splat dashed up the aisle toward the back exit.

I looked around. The Mellon brothers and Cousin Spud were heading out the same way. Apparently, at least for the moment, I'd been forgotten. It's one of my special talents. I have a magic ability to slip from people's minds. Right now, at least, I was glad to have such a skill.

I went out a side exit that led to an alley. There wasn't much of a crowd, and I found myself alone. As I started to walk toward the street, my back suddenly felt funny. It was as if I knew there was someone behind me. I spun around and looked. There was nobody there.

Then I looked lower.

I saw a man sitting in the alley, scrunched against a wall, one leg stretched out, the other folded at the knee. He was wearing faded and torn clothing. I'd walked right past him without noticing. For an instant, I tensed. Then I relaxed. I recognized him. His name was Lew. He was always hanging around town, but he never bothered anybody. Kids sometimes joked that he owned the town, since it's called Lewington.

He was looking down at the ground, or at nothing. But after I turned toward him he raised his head. For a second, he glanced my way, his eyes seeming totally without interest. Then something odd happened. As his head started to drop down, it snapped up again, and he stared at me. It was as if he'd suddenly realized that he'd seen something different from what he'd expected.

I backed up a step. "What are you looking at?" I asked.

He didn't answer. He just kept staring.

For a moment, I stared back. Then I spun away and raced out of the alley. For some reason, I felt I had to flee from him. This was his alley. I didn't belong there.

I was running.

That was not something I did very often. It was certainly not something I enjoyed.

Until now.

I was running, and it felt . . . good. I reached the edge of the alley and turned onto the sidewalk. I kept running, breathing deeply. Did I need to pant? I realized I was breathing that way out of habit. Before, whenever I'd run, I'd had to gasp for breath. But this time, my lungs didn't ache. I slowed my breathing down.

I ran. The air rushed past me as I cruised over the sidewalk and moved through town, each foot barely touching the ground. My stride was so smooth, my glasses hardly bounced.

So this was what it felt like.

I thought I could run forever.

But halfway home, I began to breathe heavily. Another block, and I began to pant. I slowed down. Then I had to stop. For a moment, I stood, unable to move. I bent over and rested my hands on my legs. After a while, I could breathe again. I walked slowly toward my house.

I wiped my forehead, then looked at my right hand. There was no sweat. That was odd — I felt hot and was still panting a bit. The cool air felt wonderful as I drew it over my tongue. Something else was wrong. It took a moment for me to notice, but once I saw it the strangeness leaped out at me. My third finger was the same length as my middle finger. I stared at the hand, then looked at the left one. It was the same way.

I was almost positive they hadn't been this way before, but there was the evidence right in front of my eyes. Maybe I was having a growth spurt.

Walking down the street, holding my hands in front of me, I realized I must have looked like someone carrying an invisible tray, or like a movie monster carrying the woman who had just fainted at the sight of him. I let my hands drop and walked the rest of the way home.

"How was the movie?" Mom asked when I came in.

"Great. Best brain-sucking leech movie ever. Brains were flowing like water. It was terrifically gross," I said. "What's for dinner?"

She sort of grinned and pointed over her shoulder with her thumb, directing my attention to the counter. There, stacked four high and six across, were aluminum food containers — the kind she used when she was catering. "You know that lamb curry you liked so much?" she asked.

"Someone cancel out on you?"

"Yup. The McKlosky wedding just turned into the McKlosky War. It seems the bride and groom discovered that they really don't want to spend the rest of their lives together. At least they figured it out before they went through with it. But the wedding is off, and I'm stuck with many gallons of lamb."

It was a good thing I liked the curry. Once, Mom had gotten stuck with eighteen pounds of chopped liver. There were a lot of happy dogs in the neighborhood that week.

I helped Mom take most of the containers down to the freezer. The smell was wonderful, and I was almost drooling with hunger by the time we were finished.

By then, my dad had come home from the college. He teaches chemistry there, but he's interested in everything. I guess I'm a lot like him, though he really gets lost in his thoughts pretty often, and has a hard time noticing the world.

We dined on the curry. The chunks of meat seemed especially tasty. I really wolfed my meal down. At one point, Mom even gave me a look and said, "Slow down, it's not going anywhere."

After dinner, as Dad and I were cleaning up, the doorbell rang. Mom answered it, then returned to the kitchen. "Norman," she said, seeming slightly puzzled, "there's a man to see you."

I put the dishtowel back on the hook and went down the hall. There, standing at the open door, was a man dressed in safari clothes. Something about him looked familiar.

His face — that was it. He had the same face as Husker Teridakian, the bumbling vampire hunter who had gone after Splat. But beyond the face, there was no resemblance. Where Husker had been a small man, this person at my door was at least six feet tall and built like a football player.

"Norman Weed?" the man asked, extending a hand. His voice was deep and full of confidence. This was not a man who worried about the small things in life.

I nodded and watched as my own hand vanished within his grip. I sensed that he could crush my fingers to mush if he wanted to.

"Teridakian," he said. "Zoltan Teridakian. My brother spoke to me of you. I am a hunter, also. But of another sort. I believe you can help me."

"How?" I looked in his eyes. Whatever bumbling ran through the Teridakian bloodline, this man had received none of it. He looked very competent. He looked dead serious.

CHAPTER 7

THE HUNTER

"**M**y brother has wasted his life chasing after fantasies," Teridakian said. "He seems to believe the world is awash with vampires. Even as a child, his mind ran away with him. The other children and I would hide behind trees and then jump out to scare him." He paused for a moment and smiled, as if reliving fond memories. Then he shook his head and continued. "Perhaps we shouldn't have done it. Perhaps that is why he is what he is. But I am not here to talk about my poor brother. Unlike Husker, I hunt what is real." He raised his hands, as if holding a rifle, and sighted down the barrel at me.

For an instant, I felt my body freeze. For another instant, I had the urge to slash at his hands and knock the invisible gun from his grip. My right hand started to curl into a claw. I could feel my back muscles grow tight as I prepared to lash out. But that was crazy. I shook my head. I couldn't believe I was about to slash at an invisible gun.

Teridakian lowered his hands. "I hunt what is real," he repeated. "But not what is natural. There are creatures beyond those most people are aware of — creatures of the night and of the shadows. I know they are real. Legends do not spring from thin air. Behind each myth is a reality. There is something in your town. I've seen the signs and followed trails. You, too, may have seen something. You may not even realize what it is you've seen."

"I have no idea what you're talking about," I said, struggling to keep my voice calm.

"The strange, the unusual, the unexplained," he said. "The trail has led me to your town. Others may believe there is nothing here beyond rumors and imagination, but the cause is real, very real."

I shook my head. "I still don't know what you mean."

He placed a heavy hand on my shoulder. "That does not matter for now. Just be alert. You are an observer. You see. You think. You can help me find what I seek. This will be my finest moment, my greatest challenge. I was born for this hunt." He paused and nodded his head, almost bowing. "I will be in touch with you."

With that he spun away and strode down the

steps, leaving me to stand and watch him walk off into the darkness.

As I started to close the door, I caught a glimpse of motion from across the street. Someone was crouched behind a tree on the other curb, watching me. I heard a car coming down from the corner and glanced in its direction. In the wash of the headlights, I expected to catch a better view of the watcher, but when I looked again there was nobody there.

This situation could become very bad. The last time a Teridakian had come to town, there had been all sorts of trouble. I had to tell Splat about this. "I'm going out," I called to my parents.

"Have fun. Don't be too late," Mom said from the kitchen.

"Bye," Dad called.

I went down the steps and headed for Splat's house. The next thing I saw made me wonder if I really was losing my grip on reality. Up ahead, there was a clown doing something to a telephone pole. It all looked so out of place that I closed my eyes for a moment. When I looked again, he was still there, facing the pole, leaning over. I got closer and the scene didn't change. It was a clown. He was holding a flashlight in one hand and a marking pen in the other. He was mumbling something. Before I reached the pole, he straightened up and walked down the street to the next pole. I caught some of his words and realized it wasn't the sort of language a kid was supposed to hear, and it certainly wasn't the sort of language a clown was supposed to use.

I stopped to look at what he'd done. There was a circus poster on the pole. At the bottom, in the spot that listed the big attractions, the clown had crossed out the part about the Monkey Boy. I moved ahead. With the clown stopping at every pole, the distance between us grew shorter and shorter. I passed him several poles later.

I was going to say something, but despite the big smile painted on his face, he didn't seem very happy. I guess I wouldn't be happy either if I had to walk all over town dressed as a clown, spending my evening scratching off the Monkey Boy from a couple of hundred posters. So I kept my mouth shut and went on toward Splat's house.

Angelina answered the door. She's Splat's older sister. As far as I can tell, her main reason for existence is to keep the malls in business. I mean, she's reasonably bright, and she seems to have a talent for poetry, but she's more interested in appearances than anything else.

"Oh, it's you," she said, apparently annoyed that I dared to exist. She walked away, leaving the door open.

I went up to Splat's room. He was looking at comic books with Rory, who couldn't quite read yet, but was learning to pick out a few words.

"Norman," Rory said, giving me a big smile. "I'm reading comics."

"That's great. Listen, Splat, you won't believe who I met."

"Another wolf?" Splat asked, not bothering to raise his gaze from his copy of *Swollen Rat People*.

"Nope," I said, trying to ignore his taunt, "another Teridakian."

"What?" That got his attention. The comic dropped out of his hands and fluttered to his lap.

I nodded. "This one doesn't chase vampires. He's a hunter."

"What does he hunt?" Splat asked.

"He . . ." I realized Teridakian had never told me. "I don't know."

"So what are you worried about?" he asked.

I didn't know the answer to that, either. All I could do was shrug.

"You think too much. That's your problem. Here," Splat said, pointing to a stack of comics, "help yourself."

"Thanks." I took a copy of *Ultimate Conqueror* and joined Splat and Rory in the pursuit of fine literature. As much as I love great books, sometimes there's nothing like a good comic to get your mind settled. For the moment, I actually forgot about the hunter. But this slice of regular life, reading comics with my buddies, was just about the last normal experience I would have before things turned very strange.

CHAPTER
8
FACE-TO-FACE

On the way home from Splat's house, I believe I ran again. I don't know for sure. One moment, I was walking down his porch steps, the next, I found myself near my own porch, slightly out of breath, though less winded than the last time. My skin felt chilled, as if I had been standing in a breeze or moving through the air.

There have been times when I've been deep in thought and lost track of what was happening around me. Once, when I was trying to figure out a very tricky physics problem, I actually rode my bike all the way to the park without really being aware of where I was going. Several times, I know I've walked all the way home from school without noticing where I was going.

But during those other times, I'd been thinking about stuff. This time, I couldn't recall any thoughts.

"Excuse me . . ."

The voice caught me by surprise. I let out one of my less-intelligent-sounding grunts, along the lines of "Huh?"

Someone stepped up from the shadows, moving toward the edge of the dim circle cast by the streetlight down the block, but stayed too far away for me to make out his face. "Is there a bus station in town?" he asked. He spoke slowly, as if it was difficult for him to form the words. He appeared to be about my height, but his voice was that of an adult.

"Where do you want to go?"

There was a pause, then he said, "Anywhere. Away. Just away."

I realized I'd had no business asking that question. I'd been the victim of enough curiosity to know it wasn't right to pry into the problems of another person. The thought of someone who was so desperate to leave a place that he would settle for going anywhere else — anywhere at all — was a very sad thought. He was still waiting for directions. I pointed toward the center of Lewington. "Go straight up this street for two blocks, then turn right at the corner. That will take you all the way to the middle of town. The bus station is across the street from the supermarket."

"Thank you." He walked toward me, his head down.

He was wrapped in strangeness almost as if it

were a layer of bandages he could never remove. As he went past, I felt myself grow tense. But I wasn't tensing from fear. I sensed a difference in him that made me uncomfortable. I wondered if this was the way Splat felt around insects.

The man must have sensed something, too. He stopped and turned back to face me. Then he lifted his head. At that instant, there was no doubt who he was. His hair-covered face, twisted and deformed, showed no sign of expression as he stared at me.

"You . . . you're with the circus. . . ."

"I *was* with them. I've left."

With that, the Monkey Boy resumed his walk toward the bus that would carry him away from town. I wondered what torture it must be for him, a human trapped in that small body and cursed with the disfigured face that had led him to a life in the circus. The next time I felt like complaining about some tiny problem or minor annoyance, I knew I would think of him — I would see him in my mind and be happy with my own situation.

I went into my house and up the stairs. But my body itched. I wondered if I had rolled through poison ivy when I was in the woods. That would not be pleasant. I'd only touched poison ivy once, and it had been a miserable experience. I showered, but it didn't help the itching as much as I thought it would.

As I was climbing into bed, I heard a rip. The

sheet tore where I'd pulled it, shredding beneath my grip. My nails had grown longer than I'd realized. I cut them, then went to sleep.

And ran.

I ran in my dreams. I ran along a sandy beach, staying at the very edge between water and land. It wasn't easy keeping in the middle — the water was constantly moving. But I managed. I ran along the beach and toward the moon.

To my left, the water crashed in waves upon the beach, churning, changing, flowing. To my right, the land was solid and firm. Part of me wanted to dive into the wild freedom of the water and swim away. Another part of me wanted to climb to the safety and security of high ground and stand upon the rocks that rose above the beach. I couldn't decide — to choose one way meant giving up the other — so I ran along the edge.

The moon was huge, as large in size as I was. The light seemed warm and soft. It pulled at me. I ran for miles.

When I woke, I remembered the dream. The thought excited me. My heart pounded. Mostly, I remembered that I did not run upright but on all fours. As I got ready for school, the memory of the dream faded.

Mom was always telling me that breakfast is the most important meal of the day. Sometimes I'm not hungry when I get up, but I certainly didn't argue with her that morning. I was starving. I ate a hearty breakfast, then headed off to class.

I was three blocks from school when I saw Spud Mellon walking toward me. *You don't know me*, I thought, wishing hard that he wouldn't recognize me. *You've never seen me before. You don't even see me now.* I tried to keep a calm, steady pace and act as if there was nothing wrong. He drew closer. I avoided his eyes. He was almost up to me. Then he was next to me.

I held my breath. He was behind me. I'd gotten past him. I let the breath out. Luck was with me this morning. He'd forgotten all about what I'd done in the movie. He didn't recognize me.

"Hey, I know you!" The shout blasted through me like a punch in the stomach.

I heard the grinding of the soles of his shoes on the sidewalk as he spun back toward me. "Gonna get you."

I glanced back. Spud Mellon was racing toward me, his face glowing with the anticipation of the pain he was about to inflict.

HOWL ABOUT THAT?

*T*he best I could hope for, once he caught me, was that he'd lose interest in hurting me before he did any serious damage. With luck, he'd just hit me a couple of times and then decide I was too soft and small to be much fun as a punching bag. I didn't see any way to escape. He was big and slow, but he was right behind me and I'm not a fast runner.

I gave it my best shot. I tucked my head down and pumped my arms and sprinted. Any instant, I expected to be yanked to a halt as he grabbed the back of my jacket and lifted me in the air like a small bag of pretzels.

Behind me, the sound of his footsteps grew fainter. Puzzled, I risked a glimpse back. I had actually managed to pull away from him by a half a block. I looked ahead. There was a house on the corner with a stone wall running along the front and sides of the yard. I wondered if I could gain some more distance by making a sharp turn. I shot to the left, hugging the wall. For an instant, I was out of his sight. Ahead of me, I noticed a huge oak tree by the curb to my right.

I watched this next part. I mean, I did it, but it was almost as if I just watched it happen. I ran right at the tree — straight at it. Then, and this is the only way I can describe it, I hit the trunk with one foot and then the next and I was running up the tree. I didn't run far, but my momentum carried me high enough to grab a branch. The next thing I knew, I was crouched on that branch, staring down at the street below me.

Spud came around the corner a second later. At first, he kept running, not seeming to realize that I was no longer in front of him. Then he slowed. Then he stopped. He stopped right beneath me. He stood, looking around like a dog does when you hide his favorite toy, trying to see where I had gone.

From above, I focused on the back of his neck. It would be so easy to drop down on him. I had the advantage. I could take him out before he knew what hit him. I could knock him flat with almost no effort. I could —

What was I thinking? I shook my head, trying to throw off the image of tackling this monster below me. I couldn't believe I had seriously thought about leaping on him from the tree. I wasn't even sure how I was going to get down. To tell the truth, I wasn't even completely sure I knew how I had gotten up there.

So I just waited. In a few minutes, he wandered off, muttering, "Gonna get him. Gonna get him real good. Pound him to pieces."

I held on to the branch and hung down. The ground seemed awfully far away, but I couldn't think of any other way to get out of the tree. I let go and dropped. For an instant, I was weightless. Then my feet hit. My knees bent. I absorbed the shock.

As far as I could tell, I was unhurt. None of my bones had snapped from the impact. I walked back to the corner and peeked out past the wall, making sure Spud Mellon wasn't in sight. Then I hurried to school.

The rest of the morning went by without incident. Lunch was fine, though I ate a lot more than usual. After that, things got strange.

I was on my way to class from lunch when I passed by the music room. Several kids from the band were practicing, and I stopped outside the door to listen. In some ways, music is a lot like math. Maybe that's why I like it. One of the kids was playing the clarinet. It sounded really good.

I'm not very musical, myself. That particular skill seems to have avoided my family entirely. Mom and I leave the room whenever Dad starts singing. Mom claims I started crying every time she tried to sing me a lullaby when I was a baby.

I'm no better. When they first let us learn an instrument in school, I thought I wanted to take the violin. I still remember what happened after I made my request. The music teacher, Ms. DiGamba, played a couple of notes on the piano and asked me to sing them. I guess I didn't come very close. She made this squished-up face like she had just eaten a particularly crunchy insect, then said to me, "Drums, lad, think about drums. I wouldn't suggest you venture anywhere near the violin." In other words, as much as I like listening to it, making music isn't one of my strong points.

But I couldn't help singing along that afternoon. The clarinet just made me feel good. I had to join in. Each note stroked me like a warm breeze. I really started getting into it. I was with it. I was cool. I was happening. I became the music and the music became me. Then I heard another sound mixing with the instruments and realized I wasn't alone. I was surrounded by a crowd of kids who were laughing and pointing.

"Norman is really out of his skull this time," someone said.

"Maybe it's an experiment," someone else said.

There were a few other comments of equally low wit and depth. I guess my singing must have been pretty bad. "Yeah, I was experimenting with harmonic resonance," I said. "The acoustical nature of this hallway, when compared to a typical Venturi structure, is quite enlightening." I continued to talk about the science of acoustics and the nature of sound. That did the trick.

As the crowd melted away, I noticed Splat standing there, looking puzzled. "What were you doing?" he asked.

I was about to answer when I realized I wasn't really sure. I'd thought I'd been singing, but I couldn't remember the words. "What do you think I was doing?" I asked.

"Howling," Splat said.

"Howling?"

He nodded. "Like a dog. Normy coyote. Just howling along." He grinned, then went, "Awwwooooooooo."

"Are you sure I wasn't singing?" Try as I might, I couldn't remember what I had sounded like. I just knew I was singing out my soul along with the clarinet.

"Positive. Believe me — you definitely weren't singing." He laughed, then he stared at me and said, "You look different. Did you get a haircut or something?"

"Nope. No haircut." I ran my fingers through my hair. It didn't feel any different than usual.

Splat shrugged. "Well, something looks different."

The bell rang, and we hurried off to math class. Here was something safe and familiar. In that room, at least, everything made sense. I knew I could always count on numbers. Two times two would always be four, even if the rest of the world was getting stranger and stranger. Add two odd numbers and you get an even number, guaranteed. Multiply a number by zero and the result is zero, every time. It doesn't change. Numbers never let you down.

We had a test. I sat and did the problems that were written on the board, getting lost in the safe universe of mathematics. Most of the time I didn't even need paper to work out the math. The answers were there for me. I wasn't showing off — it was just something I was good at.

"Norman?"

I looked up. Mr. Phermat, the math teacher, was standing at my desk, staring down at me.

"Yes?"

"Do you need to go to the nurse?" he asked.

"Pardon me?" I had no idea what he was talking about.

"You've been scratching all afternoon," he said. "I thought you might have poison ivy or something."

I looked at myself. In one hand, I held my unused pencil. The other hand was scratching my chest. As I glanced down, I noticed something else that I hoped my teacher hadn't seen — my shirt was filled with small rips and slashes. They weren't obvious from a distance, but I'm sure they hadn't been there before.

"I'm fine," I said, looking back up and trying to draw his attention away from my hand. "It's just a nervous habit, I guess. I was noticing an interesting pattern in the numbers from the first five problems. Look, see that thirty-seven in the first one. Now, the second problem has a seventy-four, which, of course, is twice thirty-seven. Now, that's just a coincidence, and I'm sure there was nothing intentional on your part when you constructed the test, though we do have to consider the role of the subconscious. However, and this is quite amazing, if you look at the numbers in the third problem —"

"Very nice, Norman," Mr. Phermat said, backing away from my desk. "Better get on with your work, though." He walked up the aisle. As he reached his desk, he looked back at me and said, "Something's different. . . . I know, you got a haircut."

He turned away before I could say anything. I put one hand on the desk and tried to make sure it stayed there while I wrote with the other. Even so, I caught myself scratching more than once before the end of the class.

What was happening? I looked at my shirt. It was actually shredded. I remembered spilling some chemicals on it last week while doing an experiment. That must be it — the chemicals had weakened the cloth.

That explanation satisfied me. It's always best to go with the simplest solution. At least, it satisfied me for a while. But after what happened in gym class, I began to realize that my life had taken a turn down a path where there were no simple solutions.

TO THE MAT

I won't say that I hate gym class. I understand the importance of exercise and physical fitness. But surely exercise could be more pleasant than they make it in school. This month, it was especially unpleasant. We were wrestling. There are few things I find less delightful than being folded up into a human pretzel by one of my sweaty classmates. My neck was not designed to be wedged behind my knees; my ankle was not meant to be pressed into my ear.

Imagine my surprise when, barely three seconds after starting my bout against Ernest Gabrielli, I found myself pinning him to the ground. I had no idea how I had done it. From the expression on his face, Ernest was also clueless. Mr. Bersicker, the gym teacher, who was standing there with his whistle dangling from his neck — apparently after the whistle had fallen from his still-open mouth — didn't seem to know what had happened, either.

I remember that he had blown the whistle for us to start the match. Then Ernest, who was about my size but a lot stronger, had stepped forward to grapple. And I had met him. In an instant, we'd ended up on the ground. I'd pinned him flat.

For a moment, I didn't move. I was almost trembling with the rush of excitement that came from victory. I stood reluctantly, backed away, and let my prey rise. *Prey?* Where did that thought come from? I mean, I let my opponent up.

I stumbled off the mat and joined the rest of the class on the floor. Nobody said anything. I'd bet nobody really believed what they had just seen. I almost didn't believe it myself. If you drop a penny a billion times, it might land on its edge once or twice. That's about how likely it was that I could pin someone, especially that quickly. I could whip anyone in the school on any kind of test, as long as it involved nothing more physical than writing answers on paper. But in the real world, the world of strength and power, I was usually a spectator or victim.

As we were leaving the gym at the end of class, Mr. Bersicker looked at me and asked, "New haircut?"

I shook my head. In the locker room, when I looked for my glasses, it hit me — I hadn't been wearing them. That's why Splat and everyone else thought I'd looked different. They knew something had changed, but hadn't figured out what it was. I hadn't really noticed, either. I'd left the house without my glasses, and the world wasn't blurry.

Things had changed. I could see in dim light, and I could hear much better than before. What else? "Be rational," I said out loud. "Be a scientist."

Kids around me stared, but I ignored them and grabbed a notebook. I started listing the symptoms — the running, the climbing, the hunger, the dreams, and on and on. Then I listed as many possible causes as I could for each symptom.

Only one cause appeared in every single column.

Around me, the others had left the locker room, but I stayed and stared at the list. There it was — right in front of my eyes. I could no longer hide from the reality that was slapping me in the face with one strange incident after another. Until now, I had forced myself to ignore the evidence. I had been a bad scientist, refusing to accept the facts because they led to a conclusion I didn't want to reach. But there was only one answer that fit.

I was becoming a werewolf.

I couldn't hide from the truth any longer. I had to deal with the situation. And I didn't think I had a lot of time. From what I'd seen or read, a werewolf was strongest during the full moon. It was then that he became entirely a wolf and ran through the night out of control, no longer in touch with his human side.

I thought about the date. The full moon was less than a week away. There was no way of knowing what would happen then, but I suspected it would, at the very least, be an experience beyond anything I had encountered before. Still, I couldn't imagine ever losing all control. I was a thinking animal, not a beast. That could never change. I closed the notebook and hurried back to my classroom.

What next? I needed to gather more facts. The thought of doing research excited me. The day dragged by, but finally my last class ended.

As I left school, I considered running home to my computer and posting a question on the Net. Surely someone out there had information that could help me. But the Net was far from private. I would be leaving a trail if I did that. I would be jumping up and down and shouting, "Hey, here I am!"

I decided to begin my research the old-fashioned way. Lewington had a decent library. It wasn't as large as the one in the capital, but it was a good start. I walked into the center of town and up the stone steps to the front entrance of the building. They'd put the whole catalog on computer several years ago. After a quick search by subject, I found that there was actually a book about werewolves, and it was not currently checked out. It was in the psychology section, down in the basement of the old part of the library.

The musty smell of old books greeted me as I reached the bottom of the steps. Rows of shelves, shoved close together, filled all the available space. It was a fabulous storehouse of information. I found the area I wanted and looked for the book.

But it wasn't on the shelf. I stood staring at a space right where it should have been, feeling an eerie sense that I was seconds too late. Had the book been a person, I suspect the opening would still have been warm.

"Looking for this?"

I spun around. There was Lew, the homeless guy, holding out a book in one hand. I backed off a step, feeling trapped amid the shelves. I didn't like feeling trapped — I didn't like it at all. Something short and harsh shot from my throat. It was a snarl. I couldn't believe I had just snarled.

"Easy, boy," Lew said. He backed up a step. "I just wanted to keep you from wasting your time. Most of this is nonsense. You'd get more information from the Sunday comics or Saturday morning cartoon shows. Chapter three's got a few half-right bits of information, but the rest is useless hogwash."

He tossed the book to me. I shot out my right hand and caught it.

Lew backed up another step, but kept his eyes locked on mine. I finally looked away. It wasn't fear on my part. It wasn't anger or hate on his part. I just knew I had to turn my eyes from his. He'd won some sort of contest. I didn't know what the rules were, but there was no doubt that he'd won.

"Come see me when you're ready for the truth," he said. "But don't wait too long." Then he slipped away toward the stairs, leaving me holding the worn volume of werewolf lore.

As I watched him move off, my mind flashed back to that encounter in the woods. The gray creature that had attacked me in the clearing — it had moved the same way. My hand rose and touched the spot on my nose where I'd been bitten.

My instinct was to run after him, to stop him and ask the questions I needed to ask. But I couldn't. For the first time in my life, I wasn't sure if I was ready to hear the truth. Instead, I took the book to a table, sat down, and started reading chapter three.

A WOLF IN CHEAP CLOTHING?

The chapter was called "Myth or Reality," and it discussed what might or might not be real about werewolves. It wasn't all that rare, according to what I had read, for a person to think he was a werewolf. It also wasn't uncommon for someone to think he was Elvis or Napoleon. But I was obviously not imagining all of this.

Of course, if I was imagining it, how would I know? What evidence did I have? I thought back. I had done some strange things in the last few days, beginning with falling out of the window. That certainly wasn't the smartest move I'd ever made.

I closed the book as a wave of uncertainty washed over me. *Was it all in my mind?* Had I pushed my brain so far and so hard in so many different directions that it had finally shot off in a direction I would never have anticipated? What proof did I have? I thought carefully about everything that had happened. After a while, I had to conclude that I had no proof at all.

I walked through the library, confused and concerned. If I was imagining things or believing things that weren't real, I needed some kind of help.

It was obviously impossible for me to come to any conclusion by myself. No matter what happened, how could I know it wasn't my imagination? I needed to get an opinion from someone else.

I had to talk to Splat. He knew monsters. And he knew me. That made him the perfect choice. I went out the door and started down the steps.

Lew was sitting at the bottom. He turned as I came by. "Find anything interesting?" he asked.

I shook my head.

"Starting to doubt it all, I'd bet. That's natural, if I remember. But you'll change your mind. You'll believe." He stuck his hand into a pocket of his pants and took out an old wallet. Then he pulled something small and shiny out of a compartment in the wallet. "When the moment of choice comes, you'll want to have this." He reached toward me.

I felt something the size of a silver dollar slide down to the bottom of my shirt pocket. As I glanced at Lew's hand, I noticed something inside the wallet — a worn and dirty driver's license from out of state. It was a Pennsylvania license with Lew's picture —

much younger than now — and the name *Lewis Morton* printed beneath the picture.

"You can thank me later, kid," he said. Then he spun quickly from me and jogged down the street.

I reached into my pocket and pulled out the object. It was a coin of some sort. No, not a real coin — there was no value stamped on it. It was a token, or maybe a talisman. On one side, there was the head of a wolf. I turned it over. On the other side, there was the head of a man.

"This is crazy," I said. Before I could decide what to do with it, I heard a voice behind me.

"Hey — it's that kid. Gonna get him."

I looked back. Spud Mellon, three blocks away, had spotted me. I could hear him talking to himself. I dropped the coin back in my shirt pocket and dashed down the street, turning quickly at the corner.

As I went around, I heard something else. There was a clink and a scraping metallic sound. I jammed my fingers in my pocket and saw that the cloth was filled with rips. Behind me, I caught a flash as the token rolled under a clump of bushes. I started to go back for it, but the sound of footsteps spurred me on. I raced away, cutting up the next street. Then I stopped and listened. Spud had lost track of me. I stayed where I was a few more minutes, then continued toward Splat's house. The token could wait. I'd get it later.

I hadn't walked half a block before I saw something that stopped me in my tracks. Ahead, his back to me but unmistakable, was Teridakian. He was talking to someone who was wearing a shirt that said THE HULL BROTHERS' CIRCUS.

I had no trouble hearing what they were saying.

"So we understand my price?" Teridakian asked.

"Yes. That is not important to me. As long as I have a specimen for the sideshow," the circus man said.

"You will have him," Teridakian said. "I am close. He is here. You will have him. I never fail."

"Unharmed?"

"Of course."

I crossed the street, then went past them. For some reason, I didn't want Teridakian to notice me. Another block and I stopped again. I was walking past Big Ben's Barbecue when the smell of ribs grabbed me and dragged me inside. Before I knew it, I was walking out again with my very own bagful of Big Ben's Jumbo Back Rib Bargain. I ate as I walked, burying my face in the crisply charred hunks of meat.

My hands were so full of sauce and grease that I used my elbow to ring Splat's bell.

"Hey, Norman, come in," he said when he opened the door.

"Thanks." I went right to the kitchen and washed my hands.

Angelina, who was sitting at the table painting her nails, had to make a comment. "Well, he's a nerd, but at least he's clean," she said. She frowned, then added, "And I do believe he actually got a haircut."

"I need to talk to you," I told Splat.

"Okay, but come downstairs. I have something cool to show you." He opened the door that led to the basement and headed down.

I realized he wouldn't pay any attention to me until after he showed me whatever it was he thought was so interesting. I followed him to his father's workshop. Splat's dad made jewelry. "Check it out," Splat said, picking something up from a table. He turned and tossed an object toward me.

As the object spun and glittered, I was suddenly filled with an unbearable sense of terror. I jumped aside, slamming into the wall. The object went past me and dropped to the floor, making a ringing tinkle against the concrete.

"Hey, relax, it's just a letter opener," Splat said, stepping over and picking it up. He held it out for me to see. "Look, it's not even sharp." He pressed his thumb against the side of it. "Dad just designed it the other day. Look at the handle."

I stared at the letter opener. It was made of silver. A silver bullet could kill a werewolf. So could a silver knife or a silver club. Other than the fact that it could bring an end to my existence, I had to admit that it was a nice piece of work. The handle was in the shape of a coiled snake, and there was a design etched onto the blade.

"Here." Splat held it toward me.

"That's okay." I backed away.

"What's going on?" he asked.

I looked around at all the silver in the workshop. "Can we go upstairs?"

Splat shrugged. "Sure."

We went up to the kitchen, then up the next floor to his room. "I think I'm a werewolf," I said, not knowing any way to ease slowly into the subject.

Splat cocked his head to one side then the other, making a big show of examining me. Then he shook his head. "Nah, you're Norman." He pointed to the movie poster of Lon Chaney, Jr., on his wall — the one from *The Wolf Man*. "Now *that's* a werewolf."

"I'm serious," I said.

"Let's hear a growl," Splat said.

"I'm not joking," I said. I pointed at my face. "What about this?"

Splat shrugged. "What's a haircut got to do with it?"

"I DIDN'T GET A HAIRCUT!" I gritted my teeth until I calmed down, then said, "I'm not wearing glasses. See?"

Splat nodded. "Cool, your mom let you get contacts."

"Look, Splat, I'm not kidding. I'm a werewolf."

Another voice came from behind me. "I believe you."

I turned. It was Rory. He was standing in the hall outside the room, holding a couple of his toy soldiers in one hand and a dump truck in the other.

"Thanks."

"This is crazy," Splat said.

"I've considered that possibility," I said. "I thought you could help me figure it out. There must be some way to tell for sure."

He shrugged. "What do we know about werewolves?"

"You can kill them with silver," Rory said, apparently eager to show off his knowledge.

"I'd hate to prove that the hard way," I said. "There must be some other test."

"We could wait for the full moon," Splat suggested.

"I'm not sure I should wait. I have a funny feeling that I'd better find out as much as I can before then. And that's not the only problem." I told him about Teridakian.

"This is all oddly familiar," Splat said.

"Maybe to you," I told him, "but it's all new to me." I was about to say more when we were interrupted by the sound of footsteps coming up the stairs. A moment later, Splat's dad stuck his head into the room.

"Hi, kids. Guess what? I'm taking you all to the circus. You're invited, too, Norman." He stared at me for a moment, then added, "Nice haircut."

"Wow!" Rory shouted. He started jumping around in that special dance that excited little kids have.

"Great, Dad," Splat said. He turned to me. "You coming?"

I hesitated. There was so much going on that I really wasn't sure what to do. But, then again, maybe I needed to take my mind away from all of this for a while. Perhaps a little fun entertainment would be just what I needed. "Sure, thanks," I said. After all, what could possibly go wrong at a circus?

We piled into Splat's dad's car and went across town to a field where the Hull Brothers had set up their tents. It was an all-guy trip. Splat's mom was out somewhere. Angelina decided not to come, which was a perfect decision as far as I was concerned. She felt that animals should not be used to entertain people. I didn't agree with her, but I could respect her opinion. On the other hand, she did have a cat of her own, and I really didn't see why someone else couldn't have a tiger if she could have a house cat.

As we climbed out of the car, I noticed that the animal smell was very strong. It wasn't only one smell — I could separate it into different parts. Just like in a bakery where the smell of bread might mix with the smell of chocolate, here I could sense horse and elephant and other animals. Each had its own scent.

"Cool," Splat said as we headed for the main tent. "They've got a sideshow over there. Come on."

"Not me," Rory said, staring at posters with gigantic pictures of the Snake Lady, the Human Pincushion, and the Elastic Man.

"You boys go ahead," Splat's dad said, handing us money for the sideshow. "Rory and I will look around out here."

"Great," Splat said, running toward the entrance.

I caught up with him, and we paid our admission. Then we stepped inside. The thin canvas walls of the tent separated two different worlds. Outside, everything was bright and alive. Inside, all was gloomy and sad. Even the grass beneath our feet seemed half dead.

In front of me, just sitting watching the crowd, was Fatima, the Bearded Lady. She was, indeed, a lady with a beard. Whether the whiskers were real or glued on, I felt it was wrong of me to stare at her. I moved deeper into the tent. At each spot, some person sat or stood on display, letting the crowd gawk and marvel at a deformity or oddity.

I looked around at the people pushing their way from exhibit to exhibit, and found myself wondering who the real freaks were. Next to me, a boy was stuffing popcorn in his mouth, talking loudly between crunches. This was more gruesome than anything I had paid to see. Near him, another boy stuck his finger in his nose and then in his mouth.

I hurried away from them, moving still deeper into the tent. I went past the Human Pincushion and Rinaldo, the Fire-Eating Man, and a half dozen others, until I found myself at the very end of the sideshow. A faded sign announced that this was the spot where one could see the Monkey Boy.

The cage was empty. Nothing stood on the other side of the thick bars but a lingering scent that was totally human. For a moment, as I looked at the straw-covered floor, I had the strangest sensation that I was standing inside, that I was trapped forever to live within and be stared at by a crowd who didn't know that they themselves were the freaks.

I turned, wanting to flee from the tent. Two steps and I ran into someone. It was the man I had seen talking to Teridakian. "Easy there, boy," he said, moving back from me. "You could get hurt running like that. Don't want no injuries. Nope." He looked toward the empty cage. "Yup, lost the old Monkey Boy, we did. Going to miss the little fellow. Need a replacement."

He stopped and stared at me for a moment. "Maybe you're circus material," he said, giving me a huge wink. "Want a job? We could call you the Human Boy."

"No thanks," I said, stepping around him.

I rushed toward the exit, pushing my way through the crowd, desperate for a breath of fresh air. Behind me, I could hear the circus man laughing as if he had just made the greatest joke in the world.

I waited outside until Splat emerged. "Wow, do you believe all that?" he asked. "I'd bet most of those things were fake. They couldn't be real. But that guy with the pins in his body — that sure looked real. How'd he do that?"

"I don't know." I hadn't looked closely at any of it.

"Well, boys, we'd better get some seats," Splat's dad said as he came up to us with Rory. "The show is about to start."

"Up front," Rory said. "Okay, Dad?"

"Sure," his dad said.

So we made our way to a row near the front and sat and waited for the show to start.

After a while, the music blared from speakers hung around the tent and the parade began. The clowns marched past us first, waving and smiling. One ran up and squirted Rory with water from a plastic flower on his bright orange jacket. The acrobats went tumbling by next.

After that, the horses came prancing out, stepping proudly in time with the music. I think I sensed there would be trouble an instant before it happened. The horses stopped dead when they got near our side of the ring, refusing to go past. Their nostrils flared and their eyes rolled back in terror, showing nothing but white. Something in that look of fear made me want to leap on them. I gripped the bench with both my hands and forced myself to remain seated.

I could see the trainer getting worried. Finally, he urged them to move, but they swung wide of where we sat. The performing dogs turned and started growling at me. I felt my face grow red. People were staring. The trainers finally got the dogs past. The rest of the animals also went wide to avoid me.

I glanced across the tent. On the other side, standing and staring at me, was the man from the sideshow. The one I had run from. I looked right into his eyes, and I was sure that he knew what I was. And I was sure that I was going to end up in a cage in a sideshow, howling like a wolf and throwing myself against the bars while the public stood on the other side and discussed whether I was real or a clever fake.

I knew. And I had no idea what I could do to save myself.

CHAPTER 13

RABBIT TRANSIT

I guess everyone else enjoyed the show. Rory seemed to have a real good time. Splat was pretty easily amused by anything. And his dad was the type who was always happy when his kids were having fun. So the whole male portion of the Claypool family had a good trip. As for me, I just wanted to get out of there. I did remember to thank Splat's dad for taking me. But I was glad to get back to my home.

"Have fun?" Mom asked when I came inside.

"Yeah." I smelled lamb. "Curry again?"

"Getting tired of it?" she asked.

"No, I don't mind." Actually, the thought of a nice big hunk of lamb made my mouth water. I realized I was starving.

"Where are your glasses?" Mom asked.

"You noticed?"

"Of course," she said.

"It's an experiment," I told her, feeling glad that she, at least, had actually known what was different.

"Well, just be careful you don't walk into anything."

"I'll be careful."

"Could you set the table?" Mom asked. "That is, if you can see well enough to find the forks."

"Sure."

"The everyday stuff is still dirty. Just use the good silver."

"Uh . . ." I looked in the drawer to make sure. There were no knives and forks. The utensils from last night's dinner were still in the dishwasher. The only other set we had was silver. I had images of the knife slowly burning a hole through my hand. "I'll wash them," I said, grabbing a handful of stainless steel from the dishwasher.

Mom stared at me while I cleaned several knives and forks. "Well, this is a surprise," she said. "And a pleasant surprise, I might add."

"Just trying to be helpful." *Was it in my mind?* I wondered. I went over and opened the drawer where Mom kept the silver. I reached in and touched a knife. At first, it felt warm. Within a few seconds, it got hot. I pulled my hand back. If this was all in my mind, I had a pretty powerful imagination. If it wasn't in my mind, I had a pretty powerful problem.

Dad was working late, so he wouldn't be joining us for dinner. Mom brought out the food and we ate.

Then I went up to my room. I was beyond caution by this time. I had to find out as much as I could as quickly as I could. I logged onto the Net, went to the interest group for the supernatural, and posted a question about werewolves. In a few hours, there was at least a small chance I might get some kind of useful information.

I went to bed, and thought I went to sleep. But then I woke and I wasn't me. I was a predator — something between wolf and human. I needed to run, to chase my food, to travel across the land. I snuck downstairs and out the door. I must have still had arms at that point. But it wasn't me. This was not Norman who was racing through the backstreets of Lewington. I almost felt like I was watching myself. I ran. It might have been on four paws. It might have been on two legs. I don't remember.

Rabbit!

Near me. Knows. Frozen. Fear. Where? Stop and smell. There. Don't run. My one small human spark wanted to warn it. Don't run and you might survive. Run and I will follow.

It ran. A flash of white, up, down, lop, hop, run. I had no choice but to chase. Glad. Free. Running. Rabbit smell, fear smell.

Chase.

Leap and catch.

Mine.

I held it in something midway between a hand and

a paw. It wriggled for an instant, then stopped. It knew the laws of the chase. There are rules for prey. I held it up toward the near-full moon and howled a cry of joy and triumph.

A human jolt shot along my arm to my brain. Or maybe it went the other way. I relaxed my grip. The rabbit dropped. It landed softly but remained frozen, waiting, trembling.

"Go, scat!" I spoke. Words. Human tools. "Get away."

It ran. I looked aside for a moment so I wouldn't be forced to chase the fleeing prey, then looked back. It was gone.

I turned and loped back home. I went inside to my bed, lay on top of the sheets, and shivered. What was I? The beast wrestled with the boy. The time was close. The moment of decision. What did that mean? Where had I heard those words?

I slept.

The rising sun woke me. The memories rushed back, but I was unsure if they were real or dreams. I looked at my hand. There were several loose hairs on my fingers — short white hairs, like rabbit fur.

From below, words drifted into my room. "Time to get up, Norman. You don't want to be late for school."

Somehow, all of that seemed unimportant.

What was I thinking?! How could school be unimportant? It was the only thing I was really good at.

My grades, my tests — that's who I was. I got dressed and went down for breakfast.

Mom had left a plate of pancakes for me before running off on an errand. Dad was at the table sitting by a cooling bowl of oatmeal, giving all his attention to a book that lay open in front of him.

"Dad," I said when I had joined him at the table, "I'm different."

He looked up from his book and smiled. "Of course you are, Norman. We all are. That's what makes humans so wonderful — our diversity. That is what we should celebrate and cherish." He turned his attention back to his book.

I was about to try to explain what I meant. But in my mind, I could hear myself telling him that I was a wolf. While I was sitting there, trying to think of any way of bringing up the subject, he snapped his book shut and said, "Good golly, I'm going to be late for my lecture. By the way, nice haircut."

With that, he dashed off, leaving me alone with my breakfast. As I crunched into a piece of bacon, my mind filled with the image of a struggling rabbit.

The bacon tasted wonderful.

CHAPTER 14

PLANT PROBLEM

I was almost afraid to go to school. There was no way to know what I might do. At least we didn't have gym today, so I wasn't in danger of tossing anyone across the room or accidentally removing the head of one of my classmates. I don't think I could talk my way out of that one. What could I say? "Gee, look at the interesting sheathing of nerves surrounding the vertebrae. Wow, heads really are fascinating. Notice the structure of the arteries? Fascinating . . ."

Once inside the building, I also made sure to avoid walking past the music room. Foolishly feeling that I had sidestepped any possible problems, I headed into my science class. I noticed that a couple of the kids were carrying boxes, trays, or big pieces of poster board. It must have been their biology projects. I'd done mine several weeks ago, of course, as soon as it had been assigned.

"Check it out," Danny Wilkins said, holding up a box. I peeked inside. There were several animal skulls lying on the bottom. He'd pasted labels in front of them. "My dad and I find these on the road by our house all the time." There was a sign on the front of the box: ANIMALS THAT DON'T KNOW HOW TO CROSS THE ROAD.

He put the box on the table next to some of the other projects. Just then, Dawn came rushing in, carrying a big tray with plants on it. There was a sign in front saying: POISONOUS PLANTS WITH ANIMAL NAMES. I was impressed by her linking of toxic nature and nomenclature.

"Hi, Norman," she said. "You look very mature without your glasses."

"Thanks. Nice project," I said. I took another look at it. In front of each pot there was a smaller sign: ELEPHANT EAR, FOXGLOVE, WOLFSBANE.

Wolfsbane! As I stared at the plant, something seemed to push me back. I felt a force shoving me away. At the same time, I was suddenly violently ill. It felt as if I had jammed a finger down my throat. No, make that a hand. Yikes, make that an arm. I ran from the room, trying not to throw up.

Just outside the door, I crashed into Splat. He was carrying a box full of pieces of moldy bread and cheese. The label said: HOW TO GROW MOLD.

"You have to help me," I told him.

"Sure," he said, looking slightly amused.

"Dawn's project. She brought in wolfsbane. I can't go near it. You have to get rid of it."

"That again? Come on, Norman, the wolf thing is getting pretty tiring. How about pretending you're a mummy or something for a change? You'd look good in white."

"Please."

He sighed, then said, "I'll see what I can do."

I watched him walk into the room. Then I heard him yell, "Oops!" and stumble into the table.

An instant later, there was the crash of a clay pot hitting the floor. An instant after that, I heard Dawn shout, "Sebastian! Look what you did."

"I'm sorry. I didn't mean to break it."

There was some more skittering around and other sounds. Then Splat came out of the room carrying a garbage can. "You owe me," he said as he took the can down the hall.

I walked back toward the room. Ms. Clevis met me as I was coming in the door. "You shouldn't let the animal skulls bother you like that, Norman," she said. "It's just part of nature — nothing to be afraid of."

"But I wasn't . . ." I stopped. Maybe it would be better to let her think I'd run from the skulls. "You're right, it was a silly reaction. I should just confront my fears." I walked back up to the table and stared at the skulls for a moment, then turned to her and said, "Yes, I see what you mean. These are certainly fascinating samples. Notice how the mandible on this one is much more extended than on the other, while the occipital lobe —"

"Yes, Norman, very true. Now, you'd better take your seat so class can start." She backed away from me and went to her desk.

I turned from the skulls. They were pretty interesting. But part of my mind suddenly jumped not to the wonder of biology, but to the thought of fresh meat lying on the roadside. Hunting was better, but sometimes it was necessary to scavenge.

Scavenge? Where'd that thought come from? I managed to push those images from my mind when Ms. Clevis began talking. But in a moment, something else intruded on my thoughts. If I'd had my choice, I'd sit in the front row. But we'd been given assigned seats at the start of the year. That was about to become a problem. In the seat ahead of me, Bud Mellon was leaning back in his chair — leaning far back. His head was almost over my desk. He was in my space. He was poaching on my territory. I had to defend it.

My hand curled into a claw. I hauled back and slashed across at the head of the invader.

He rocked forward just as my hand ripped past. My slashing blow streaked through the empty spot where his head had been a second ago. I nearly fell off my seat with the momentum.

"Norman," Ms. Clevis said, pausing in her lecture to stare at me. "Is something wrong?"

"A bee," I said. "I was trying to hit a bee." I looked across the room. "There it goes, out the window. It was probably the honeybee, you know, *Apis mellifera*. It's really a fascinating insect. I shouldn't have acted aggressively toward it, since by nature it is well known to be docile and —"

"Thank you, Norman. Now, as I was saying . . ." Ms. Clevis resumed her lesson.

That was close. I hadn't been sure whether I could pull it off twice in a row, but my magic was still there. I sunk down in my chair, trying to get control, hoping no one else would invade my space. This would not do. I was a rational human being, not some sort of animal that had to defend its territory.

I looked at the clock. Still two hours until lunch. I hoped they had something good. I hoped they had something with a lot of meat in it. I needed to sink my teeth into something warm — blood warm — and juicy.

"**Y**ou're turning into a real pig, you know."

"Mfffffllup." That was the best response I could make between bites. But I guess Splat was right. I paused and looked down at my hands, which were clenching the burger so tightly the meat was squishing out of the bun. It was my third.

"And Dawn is probably never going to speak to me again," he said, looking across the cafeteria to where she sat with her friends.

I stopped eating long enough to say, "She wasn't exactly chewing your ear off with conversation before this. At least you got her attention today." I paused to tear off another piece of burger. I swallowed it, then said, "But I appreciate what you did. I couldn't get near that wolfsbane."

Splat put his own burger down and looked at me. "You really are serious about this, aren't you?"

"Come on — you of all people should be a believer." Splat had been through an adventure of his own. He should certainly have no trouble accepting what I told him. I shoved the back of my hand in front of his face. "Was I this hairy before?"

He pulled his head away from my hand. "I don't know. Your body hair isn't something I keep track of."

"What about this?" I scraped my nails across the top of the table. Wood shavings came off in curls as if my fingers were chisels. "And this?" I reached in my pocket and pulled out a dime. There was enough silver in it to hurt my fingers. I let it sit on my open hand for as long as I could stand, then turned my wrist so the coin dropped to the table. I held the evidence in front of Splat's face. There, on my palm, was a red mark from the coin.

"Is this some kind of science trick?" Splat asked. "Did you have some sort of chemical on the dime?"

I shook my head. "No trick."

Splat looked right into my eyes, but there was no challenge in his stare — just realization. I could tell he finally believed me. "What are you going to do?" he asked.

"I don't know. But I have a funny feeling I need to do something soon. I'm losing control. The full moon is getting close. If it hadn't been for that stupid class trip —"

I stopped. Suddenly, though I didn't want to face it, I knew what I had to do.

"I have to go back," I told Splat.

"Back? Where?"

"The woods. I have to find the wolf. I have to talk to him."

"Talk to him?" Splat shook his head. "You're crazy. You're absolutely —"

"Stop it!" I held up my hand, cutting his words off. "Stop doubting me and start helping me. I've never asked you for anything before. Come with me. Please?" I waited for his answer.

Splat nodded. "Yeah, I'll come with you."

I knew that, no matter how much he might be wrapped up in his own interests, I could count on him when I really needed help. Maybe that's why I put up with the rest of it.

"Thanks," I said.

"When do you want to go?"

"Right after school."

"How do you know it will be there?" he asked.

"I don't know for sure," I said. But even though I didn't know, I had a strong feeling that the wolf would be there when I went back.

The day dragged on. All I could think of was getting to the woods. I hoped to face the wolf and learn something. I also wanted to run free among the trees. I could close my eyes and almost feel the wind against my face and the branches stroking my fur as I raced across a bed of fallen leaves.

I was shaken from those thoughts when I went to

math class. I realized something was wrong the moment Mr. Phermat handed back our tests. He stopped by my desk and looked at me with an expression I had never ever gotten from a teacher. Actually, I'd gotten it a lot from gym teachers, but not from any other teacher. It was an expression of disappointment.

"I hope this isn't the start of a trend," he said as he put the test on my desk.

I looked at the paper. It must have been worse than I thought. He'd actually laid it facedown. I turned over the paper and felt a jolt run through my body.

"Sixty-three?" I said out loud, unable to believe the glaring red number that was scrawled across the top of the page. "It can't be." I'd never gotten less than a ninety on a math test. I usually got a hundred. A sixty-three was not possible.

I stared at the sea of red circles and shook my head. Stupid mistakes. I'd made dozens of stupid mistakes. Where had my mind been?

Splat leaned over from his seat and looked at my test. *"Blam,"* he said. "The legend dies."

I folded the test and put it in my backpack. This won't happen again, I promised myself. Somehow, I'd slipped. The wolf in me had taken over at the wrong time. But I was sure my mind was strong enough to keep it from ever happening again. Now, more than ever, I was eager to go back to the woods.

When school let out, Splat and I rushed home for our bikes and headed toward Miller Forest. Riding felt almost as good as running, though I missed the slap of my feet against the ground. We reached the entrance, chained the bikes in the parking lot, then headed down the trail.

Walking didn't feel right. I started to jog. Splat moved with me. He'd played soccer and basketball for years and had no trouble keeping up with me. We ran together, silent, and I realized I felt closer to him at this moment than ever before. I felt that I could run forever through these woods. Alone or with a friend — it didn't matter — I could run forever.

We came eventually to a familiar spot. Reluctantly, I stopped running. I looked, I sniffed. Then I left the trail and went through the woods to the small clearing.

Splat followed. We stood and waited.

The wolf came. He made no sound. One moment, Splat and I were alone in the clearing. The next, the wolf was standing at the far edge. He looked at me. Then he looked at Splat and growled.

"I think he wants you to leave," I told Splat.

"What do you want me to do?" Splat asked.

"I'll be okay. Back away slowly. Don't run. Wait for me on the trail."

"Are you sure?"

"Yeah. Thanks." I kept my eyes on the wolf. Behind me, I heard Splat moving through the woods, going toward the trail. The sounds grew fainter.

"Well?" I said, looking at the wolf.

He stood, as if waiting for something.

"Human talking to wolf doesn't work," I said, realizing the problem. "One of us has to change. I don't know how."

The wolf remained motionless.

"I don't know how," I said again. *Or did I?* Maybe I was afraid. I suspected that if I voluntarily took the true form of a beast, I might not want to become human again.

The wolf waited.

I had to learn what I could. *Be what you are,* I thought. *Surrender to it.* I relaxed and let myself change. There was no pain, no agony in the transformation. That was an invention from the movies. It was swift and far easier than I wanted it to be.

I dropped to all fours, still draped by the clothing I wore, but no longer suited to wearing it. I stepped from the pants, then pulled the shirt off with my teeth.

"Welcome," the wolf said. It was a language of sounds and gestures, spoken as much with body movement as with voice. But I understood and was able to reply.

"Why me?"

"Remember the first time we met? I was chasing a

rabbit. You got between us. Then you ran. That sealed your fate. You made the choice when you ran. Prey always chooses itself. The rabbit, the deer, they choose to be taken. I was not looking for this to happen. It took all the strength of my human side to keep from hurting you even worse. But I welcome the company if you should decide to remain."

"Decide?" I asked, grabbing at that word and all the possibilities it contained. "I have a choice?"

"For the moment. The decision must be made soon. You will know the moment when it arrives. It is different for each of us, but you will know. And you are prepared."

"No. I'm not prepared. I'm not ready for any of this. I'm just a kid."

"So was I, once." He suddenly looked around, then said, "Run with me."

I took a step, then stopped. The woods called to me. To run with the pack, to run and hunt — that was what I was born for.

"Run," he said again. "I will take you to the deer."

I could smell her. A doe — her tawny neck at the mercy of my jaw.

"Norman, I'm coming back."

There was a crashing and stumbling sound from behind.

"Do you care for this human?" the wolf asked.

At first, the question puzzled me. Why should I care for any human? Then I remembered. I had run with this human. There were ties between us. "Yes. He's my friend."

"Then I will leave before I harm him," the wolf said. He disappeared into the woods.

I stood and watched, still tempted to let him lead me to the deer. As the other wolf left, I felt some of my own animal side growing weaker.

"Oh, no!" The shout shattered my thoughts.

I spun to see Splat standing at the edge of the clearing. He froze, looking at me and at the scattered clothes. "What did you do to him?" He smelled of sorrow and anger.

I tried to answer, but the words came out as a howl.

He grabbed a stick from the ground and stepped toward me. "He was my friend!" Splat lunged toward me, swinging the stick.

My reflexes were more powerful than my control. My instinct was to fight back against any attack. It didn't matter that he was my friend. The threat had to be answered with action. I leaped toward him, a flash of fur, snarling, ready to tear him to shreds.

CHAPTER
16
SPLAT'S SURPRISE

My leap sent him flying. I misjudged the power of my legs and went tumbling past Splat as he fell. I tried to control myself, but the fury was upon me. I prepared for another jump. He reached in his pocket and pulled out a plastic bag. As I ran toward him, he frantically ripped open the bag.

I was struck by the smell, thrown back by the power of it. Splat, rising to his knees, shaking, held the wolfsbane in front of himself.

"What did you do with him?" He cried as he stepped forward.

I turned and ran, too fast for him to follow. But I didn't run far.

Carefully, silently, I moved back close enough to watch, but kept some distance between us to avoid the scent of the wolfsbane. Splat was gathering my clothes. He looked sad, deeply sad. He was shaking his head slowly. "Norman . . ." he whispered once. Then he walked away.

In the distance, I heard a howl. The wolf called to me. But my friend was off in the other direction, probably filled with sorrow over my end. I couldn't let him suffer. I had to change back.

I didn't know how.

When I'd become the wolf, it had been in the presence of another werewolf. Some of the power — maybe all of the power — must have come from him. Now, I wasn't sure what to do. My mind was less than human, more aware of the scents and sounds of the woods. The human spark within was dim.

And what a marvelous chance to learn about the animal. I knew that any naturalist on the planet would give almost anything for the opportunity to observe what I was seeing from the inside. This was a scientist's dream — seeing an animal from within its mind. This was the ultimate laboratory. The things I could learn. The advances I could make toward the understanding of lupine activity. The wonderful —

I realized I was no longer a wolf.

I was a boy, standing naked in the woods. Maybe the body of a wolf wasn't made to hold thoughts of science and logic. Treading as carefully as I could in my bare feet, I hurried toward the parking lot, hoping I could catch Splat before he left with my clothes.

He was at the edge of the lot, sitting on the ground next to the bikes, his head down.

I was about to call to him when I heard someone coming. A moment later, Dawn coasted into the lot, stopping her bike right next to Splat. Impossible as it might sound, I suddenly felt even more naked than before.

"Hi, Sebastian. What are you doing here?" Dawn asked as she leaned to her right and rested one foot on the ground. A bead of perspiration rolled down her forehead, and the scent of her washed over me. I realized, for the first time, that girls smelled much different from boys. It was not at all unpleasant.

There was no response from Splat.

Dawn tried again. "I'm sorry I got angry with you about that silly plant."

Splat didn't look up. I don't even know if he heard her.

"Want to go for a ride?" Dawn asked.

I could see her face as I peered through the bushes. She was smiling, but the smile didn't last long. Poor Splat. Now she looked angry. "Okay, be like that, you big snob." She pedaled off.

As soon as I was sure she was gone, I stuck my hand out through the branches and waved. "Hey, Splat, could you toss me my clothes?"

He stood and whirled around, his eyes so wide I thought they'd pop out and bounce away. "Norman!

You're alive. I thought the wolf . . ." An instant later, he looked as angry as Dawn. He grabbed my clothes and threw them at me. They landed all around me, dangling from the branches of the bushes like some bizarre and twisted ad for designer jeans.

I grabbed my underwear and put it on.

Splat started shouting at me. "How could you let me think you were dead? How could you do that? Here I am, all torn up about it. And Dawn — what's she going to think? How could you . . . ?" He sort of gestured and pointed and his face turned redder.

"Sorry." I pulled the rest of my clothes free and got dressed. I felt much more civilized as soon as I got everything back on. It's amazing how much difference a few square feet of material makes. "So you thought the wolf had eaten me?"

He nodded. "Yeah. That's what I thought. It made sense. You were gone. Your clothes were there."

"Quite the neat eater, wouldn't you say? Ate me right out of my clothes, bones and all, without leaving a trace."

Splat started to look angry again. I said "Sorry" again. It was nice that he cared. It felt good.

"You learn anything?" he asked.

I thought back to my brief time with the other wolf. "Apparently, I have a choice. There's some moment of decision coming up. But beyond that, I don't know what to expect."

"Was that a werewolf?"

"I think so." I didn't tell Splat who the wolf was. It wasn't my place to betray Lew's secret, even to Splat. "That's going to be me if I'm not careful."

I went over to my bike. "Pretty lucky you held on to that wolfsbane," I said, "especially considering you didn't really believe in any of this. It was all just my wild imagination, after all."

"Yeah," he agreed. "Pretty lucky."

"So why did you have it?"

He shrugged. "It just seemed like kind of a good idea."

We got on our bikes and rode to the end of the parking lot. I noticed that Splat wasn't looking toward home. He was looking down the road in the other direction. It didn't take a genius to know what he was thinking.

"Go ahead," I said.

"What?"

"Go on. Maybe you can catch up with Dawn."

"Thanks. I'll see you later." He rode off, sprinting down the road at top speed.

I went toward home more slowly, wondering how far off the moment of decision might be, and wondering what form it might take. A part of me also wondered whether I wanted to give up a gift that made me strong and powerful. I was sure I could learn to defeat the animal urges. After all, I was a thinking creature with an exceptionally capable mind.

When I got to my house, I checked the computer.

There were ninety-six replies to my question about werewolves. Before I looked at them, there was something else I wanted to check. Dad's university account includes a service with files from hundreds of magazines and newspapers. I logged on to it and, remembering Lew's license, searched for the keywords *Lewis Morton* and *Pennsylvania*.

There was one story, from nearly thirty years ago. The headline was HIGH-SCHOOL JUNIOR GETS FULL SCHOLARSHIP. It said that Lewis Morton, a junior at Liberty High School in Ridge Valley, Pennsylvania, had made history by being offered a full scholarship to study physics at the Massachusetts Institute of Technology.

I paused and let that sink in. M.I.T. was one of the finest colleges in the world. And they let Lewis Morton skip his senior year. He had to be brilliant. "That can't be the same Lew," I said. But I knew it was. Or had been . . .

I switched back to my mail and waded through the ninety-six messages, reading enough of each one to make sure there was nothing of value. Most of the stuff was the same old misinformation. There was also an invitation to join a werewolf fan club, a long poem about werewolves from someone who didn't seem to understand poetry very well, two really bad stories, five copies of the same file of werewolf jokes, and various other useless chunks of information.

Ninety-five of the messages were worthless. It

was item number ninety-six, the last file in the group, that made my blood suddenly turn cold in my veins. It was a short message:

You cast out a net and it has helped catch you. Now I know for sure. Run. It will do no good. You are mine.

Zoltan Teridakian.

I looked at the message header. The mail had been sent to me just a half hour ago. I had to do something, but I didn't know whether to stay home or to run.

The doorbell rang.

I got up from the chair, my eyes still held by the message on the screen.

Downstairs, I heard my mother call, "Norman, that man is here to see you again."

"**N**orman, are you up there?" Mom called from the bottom of the steps.

I realized she hadn't seen me come in. But that realization was pushed aside by an emotion stronger than thought. Teridakian was on my porch. He was in my territory. I knew if I stayed there, I would have to fight to defend that territory. Whatever happened, I didn't want my mother to see me doing the things I feared I might do.

Worse, my body was changing again. My left hand had grown into something halfway between human and wolf. The fingers were covered with hair and tipped with curving nails. The thumb had retracted so far, it was nothing more than a nub. I tried to change it back, but it refused to shift.

I looked out the window. The full moon was just

beginning to rise. The sight of it gripped me. I wanted to raise my head and howl a greeting.

"Norman? Are you home?" Mom was coming up the steps.

Parts of my body felt as if they were rippling. Any moment I expected to find myself in full wolf form. When that happened, there might be no way to control my fury.

I left by the window, dropping to the ground, then running across the backyard. I kicked off my shoes, enjoying the feel of the cool grass against my feet. I cut through several more yards, then headed toward Splat's house.

Some sense told me I was being followed. I hurried.

Angelina opened the door when I rang the bell. "Hello, Wolf Boy," she said.

I looked past her to Splat. "You told her?"

"I didn't mean to. I was talking with Rory and she overheard."

"Great. Wonderful. Let's take out an ad in the paper. Who else can we tell?" I stumbled into their house. "Did you alert your parents, too?"

"They're out," Splat said.

"Maybe we can help," Angelina said.

"You'd help me?" I couldn't believe she was saying that.

She smiled. "You know me. I have a soft spot for animals."

Rory came running in from upstairs. "Are you a wolf, Norman?" he asked.

"Not quite," I told him. "But sort of, I guess."

"Cool." Rory seemed impressed.

This wasn't getting me anywhere. Quickly, I told them everything I had learned. I didn't reveal Lew's identity, but just mentioned that I had talked with someone from town. As I recounted the story of Lew in the library, it struck me. "That's it," I said. "He told me later that I had what I needed. He must have meant that metal token. It's some sort of amulet."

"So you just need it with you when this moment of decision happens," Angelina said. "Then everything will be okay."

"I lost it." I couldn't believe I hadn't gone back for it.

"Where?" Splat asked.

"By the library." I remembered the tinkling sound it had made as it went hopping into a bush.

"Let's go," Splat started out the door.

We followed him from the house. I had just reached the bottom of the steps when someone shouted, "Stop right there, werewolf!"

I spun to face Teridakian. He was about ten yards away, holding a rifle like the kind that animal control people use to shoot tranquilizer darts.

"Leave me alone," I said.

"You can't do this to him," Angelina said. "He's just a kid."

Teridakian shook his head. "He is no child. He is a Wolf Boy. Look at him. He's not human anymore. He has no rights or protection. He is mine." The hunter raised the rifle.

I faced him, holding myself back, knowing that once I attacked I would be unable to stop. "Those tranquilizers won't work. Leave before someone gets hurt." My legs changed beneath me. I staggered and fell. I was more than half wolf.

Teridakian laughed. "You underestimate me. I am prepared. I added silver chloride and silver nitrate to the tranquilizing chemicals. You will sleep, dear boy, you will sleep long enough for me to take you into captivity. My greatest achievement. Zoltan the hunter is about to capture a werewolf."

I struggled to charge at him, but I was still off balance from the changes.

He pulled the trigger.

There was an explosion from the muzzle of the rifle.

At that point, things happened in slow motion. The scene seemed to take forever, though I suspect it was just an eye blink for the others.

Splat opened his mouth to shout. Angelina raised her hand to her face in shock and fear. Rory didn't move except to flinch. A blur, gray and fast, tore across the yard from my left and leaped against my shoulder, knocking me from the path of the dart.

The dart struck the gray thing.

We landed in a tangle.

It rose and growled. It — Lew — took a step toward Teridakian.

The hunter pulled a second dart from a pouch on his belt and opened his rifle.

Lew took another step, then another. He was charging.

Then he just crumpled.

I ran.

Fear, anger, and confusion clouded my path. I knew I should have stayed to help Lew. But I also knew I had to find the talisman. My body was at war with itself. I ran on legs that were, for a moment, human and then, for another moment, those of a wolf. I was rippling and shifting.

The moon, full and huge, rose higher.

I knew the moment of decision was close.

The human part of me was determined to find the talisman. But the wolf wanted to run free. Once, on the way to town, I found myself climbing a tree. Later, though the memories are vague, I believe I climbed the clock tower on the town hall. Then I remember running across rooftops.

At some point, I lost my jacket. I still had my shirt and pants, though they both were ripped.

There was no one in sight when I reached the corner next to the library. The moon hung above the building, spilling a cold glow across the ground. I ran to the bushes. Nearby, unless someone else had found it, the talisman waited for me. I dove to the ground and began searching.

My vision kept shifting from human to wolf. It would flicker rapidly back and forth, then hold one way for a moment, then flicker again.

Suddenly, I sensed the talisman. I knew it was within reach. I thrust out a paw or a hand, I'm not sure which, to clasp the object as its power pulsed at me from beneath a bush.

Before I could get it, I was grabbed.

Something took hold of my legs.

I stretched out and felt the hot metal of the talisman. My fingers closed around it.

An instant later, I was dragged out from beneath the bushes.

"I knew it was you." Spud Mellon dropped my legs and stepped back. He faced me, his fists clenched, his face lit up with a sneer of triumph.

I stood. At that instant, I seemed to be in mostly human form. But I still had the strength and fury of the wolf within me. It was no contest. I knew I could destroy him in a heartbeat. I could slash him with no effort, or toss him away like a crumpled wad of paper. *Feel my power, enemy.*

"You little punk," he said with the confidence of a bully facing a smaller person. "I told you I was gonna get you. Guess I was right."

He pulled back his arm to throw a punch.

I snarled. He had no idea what was about to happen to him. He had no clue what he was facing. It was time to show him. I prepared to leap upon my victim.

The talisman suddenly burned against my palm. In that heat, I knew there was a message.

The moment of decision . . .

This was my moment. This was what Lew had told me about. If I attacked Spud, I was choosing the way of a beast. If I gave in to my animal side, I would become the werewolf. Was that what I wanted?

Yes!

No!

What was my other choice? Maybe I should —

Tear! Attack! My nerves and muscles screamed at me. My body ached to lunge at my enemy. This was the werewolf trying to take command.

I felt my legs shift, then shift back.

Think.

That was it. *Think!* The human way. Use my mind. Use my great gift. That was my choice.

I could break him in an instant, but the act would change me forever. I would lose the part of me that I valued the most. I would throw away my gifts, the way Lew had. If I wanted to remain human, I had to use the powers of my mind.

How?

Words were my weapon. I swallowed my rage and tried to speak calmly. "Don't hit me. You might hurt your hand."

He laughed. "I'll take that chance."

I knew it was a weak effort. I had to try harder. Or I could slash out at his soft flesh and be done with it. No, not the way of the beast. The mind — I had to use my mind. "You really don't want to do this," I said. "You aren't angry at me."

"I've been wanting to do this since I saw you."

Still wrong. Calm down. I knew what to do. "Look, you are merely displaying an aggressive tendency learned as a defensive mechanism. Such phenomena are virtually —"

"Shut up, nerd."

Wrong again. Had my mind failed? How could I be doing so poorly? He was almost an idiot. I was far smarter than him. It wasn't even a fair contest. There was no way I could possibly fail to win with my superior mind.

My goodness — I almost fell to my knees as the understanding hit me. How could I have been so arrogant and blind? How could I have done this?

"I'm sorry," I said.

It wasn't the words that held his punch. I think it was the tone, the sincerity in my voice.

"What?" He stood, confused.

"I had no right to treat you that way. I had no right to think I was better or smarter. We're both people. I made a terrible mistake."

"Yeah, you sure did."

I dropped my arms and stood before him. "If it will make you feel better, go ahead and hit me. I guess I deserve it."

In my clenched hand, the talisman was so hot I

could feel my skin blister. Despite the pain, I gripped it tighter. Beneath my clothing, my body was shifting and changing, fighting from one form to another. I stood, ready and willing to take a beating. Willing to become more human than I had been before.

Spud lowered his fists. "Look, kid. I have feelings, too. Everyone in my family gets treated this way. It's not right. You shouldn't have yelled at me. Just try to be nicer next time, okay?"

"Okay."

He turned from me and took two steps. Then he looked back and said, "Nice haircut."

"Thanks."

I watched him walk off. Above his head, the moon cast a bright light across the town.

Suddenly, the heat within my hand changed to intense cold. I opened my fingers. The talisman gleamed in the moonlight. I looked at the image. The side with the man was faceup. For an instant, I could have sworn he winked.

Then the talisman exploded in my palm in a flash of cool light.

CHAPTER
19
BACK TO NORMAN

I was, at that moment, out of energy. I staggered toward home. I was nothing but a kid, graced with a bright mind, but for now just an exhausted boy whose brain was reeling from all that had happened.

"Oh, there you are," my mother said when I walked in. "That odd man was here to see you earlier, but he went away. Oh, by the way, I gave away the rest of the lamb. It turned out your father is allergic to the curry. It was making him itch and feel dizzy, and he even started seeing things. I hope you didn't have any bad reactions to it."

I shook my head, too tired to talk, then climbed the steps to my room. After calling Splat to let him know I was okay, I fell into bed and slept.

In the morning, I felt confused. Had it been real? If it had been real, it was over for me, but another had paid. I needed to see if I could help Lew. If he'd been captured, he'd be at the circus.

The world seemed blurry until I put on my glasses. That part of me was definitely back to normal.

I got dressed and rode my bike to the field that held the circus. The sideshow was open. I paid and went inside. Somehow, I would help Lew escape.

He was in the cage that had once held the Monkey Boy. The sign now read: THE RAGING WOLF MAN. It was Lew, but it was Lew hunched down and acting like an animal. In the dim light, I couldn't tell whether any of it was real.

I walked up to the cage.

He growled and jumped at the bars, scaring off a kid who was standing there. A moment later, quietly, he said, "Hey, kid, good to see you. It looks like you made your decision."

I nodded. "I'll get you out," I told him.

He shook his head. "You don't understand. I made my decision, too. This is what I want."

"But you're in a cage."

"Just during show time. Look, that Teridakian is an idiot, but the circus owner is no fool. He understands."

I was beginning to understand, too. "You want to do this, don't you?"

"Yeah. This was my choice. I was getting tired of town. I was getting tired of the life I'd been leading.

This will work out just fine. I'll travel around and get to see the country. We usually set up in a field, so I can run at night. Looks pretty good to me. And circus people, they don't mind if you're a bit, shall we say, on the odd side."

"So you're happy?"

"Pretty much. Looks like you are, too. Still, it's almost too bad you didn't go for the other choice. You would have made a great wolf."

"Yeah, I guess I would, at that. Say, did you ever get to college?"

He shrugged, but didn't seem surprised that I knew about him. "Yeah. I was there for a year. The next summer, camping up in New York State, is when I got bitten. I haven't done much heavy thinking since then."

I stuck my hand through the cage, and we shook. Then I turned and walked from the sideshow.

It all still didn't seem real to me. Lew was not the most reliable source. Had it been a fantasy caused by an allergic reaction to food? Had I imagined some of it or all of it?

As I rode through town, my vision wandered along with my thoughts. That's when I saw it. High up above the street, flapping in the breeze, my jacket hung from the top of the clock tower on the town hall. There it waved, far above where any human could reach. It seemed to wave both a greeting and a farewell. I was leaving something behind, but heading toward something more intelligent and mature. I might be the smartest kid in town, but I knew I had a lot to learn.

As I pedaled toward home, I thought of Lew. His choice made sense. So did mine.

Don't Miss

THE ACCIDENTAL MONSTERS #4:

THE GLOOMY GHOST

I'd walked about five blocks when I saw Norman in front of his house. He was standing there looking down the street like he was waiting for something. He's Sebastian's friend. But he's my friend, too. He doesn't treat me like a kid. Norman is really smart. He knows everything. Maybe he could help me.

"Norman," I called, running up to him. "Hey, Norman. I'm a ghost."

Norman took a step and walked right through me.

It was weird, because it didn't feel like anything. For a second, when his body passed through my head, I saw inside him. But it was real dark, and I think I closed my eyes. I wish I'd closed my ears. I *heard* his heart. It sounded all squishy and wet.

"NORMAN!" I called as he walked away.

He didn't stop. It was hard to remember that people couldn't hear me. I was used to being seen. I'd been visible all my life. Well, I was invisible to adults sometimes, but they could still see me if they had to. I tried again.

"NORMAN!" I shouted.

He paused and looked around, then said, "How peculiar. I appear to be having an auditory hallucination. Not unusual, considering the number of synapses in the cerebral cortex. I'm sure it's nothing to worry about."

I had no idea what that meant. "NORMAN!" I shouted again. This time, he didn't even stop or look around. He ran down the street toward the mailman who was coming this way. I guess he was waiting for a package or something.

I turned back toward the Winston House. I'm not supposed to cross the street by myself. That's one of the big rules. There are lots of rules, but only a couple of big ones. Those are the ones that, if you don't listen, you could get hurt. Don't play with matches. Don't talk to strangers. Don't get anyone in the Mellon family angry with you.

I guess the big rules didn't count right now. Even so, it felt funny walking across a street without holding anybody's hand. Then Yip ran ahead and a car came at him. I screamed. The car went right through Yip without hitting him. He wasn't hurt at all.

Even though I knew I couldn't be hurt either, I didn't want to get hit. So I raced over and grabbed Yip and hurried to the other side of the street. I guess I was really a chicken crossing the road. That made me laugh.

I kept feeling happy all the way across town, until I got close to the hill. Then I walked up the hill, watching the Winston House growing bigger and bigger. It almost looked like a little castle. There were three floors. I could tell that from the windows. One corner had a round part — I don't know what they call it. That's what made me think of a castle. The old brown paint was pretty faded, and a lot of it had fallen off. By now, I was so close I had to bend my head back to see the top of the house.

"It's daytime," I said. "Nothing scary happens in the daytime."

Boy was that a lie. Look how much had happened to me already since I got up this morning.

But I had another idea. "I'm a ghost," I said. "Nothing can hurt me. . . ."

One minute you're a kid...
the next minute you're a vampire!

THE ACCIDENTAL MONSTERS

#1

THE VANISHING VAMPIRE

by David Lubar

Splat's going completely batty!
Some weird vampire guy has
made a mistake and turned
him into a vampire! His new
powers seem cool, but soon he's
sick of avoiding sun, crosses,
and garlic, and ughh...eating
raw liver! Can't he just shake this
curse and be a normal kid again?

Available in bookstores
everywhere this September.

SCHOLASTIC

AM1497

One minute you're a kid...
the next minute you're a witch!

THE ACCIDENTAL MONSTERS

#2

THE UNWILLING WITCH

by David Lubar

Angie was just a normal kid...
until that old lady touched her in
the park. Now she's turning her
brother Splat into oatmeal—and
riding an Electric Broom! What's
worse, everyone wants to steal
her powers! Angie's weary
of witching. Can she get
to the magic place before
midnight and break the spell?

Available in bookstores everywhere this September.

AM2497